This book belongs to:

A CHILDREN'S STORY BOOK

TABBY AND TOMMY

Told and illustrated by Dolly Rudeman

*

This Series includes the following titles:

At first the terrier Tommy and the pussy-cat Tabby were not very fond of each other. It was easy to see that one did not really trust the other. Tabby thought: "What does this horrible dog with his shaggy coat want?" At the same time Tommy thought: "This naughty pussy will naturally try to steal my titbits away from me!" However, when Tommy did not do anything to tease the pussy and when Tabby left Tommy's food alone, they slowly began to have a different opinion about each other and one day Tabby said to Tommy: "How about becoming good friends?" and Tommy, who was a very peace-loving dog and all for being friendly, answered joyfully: "That would be very nice, but please stop looking so angrily at me with your green eyes!" Tabby said: "Alright, I promise you, Tommy." And from this moment on Tabby and Tommy became the greatest of friends.

One day Tabby and Tommy were playing together. It was rather a rough game, but they were enjoying it very much. Suddenly, however, Tommy called out: "Tabby, what has happened?" and mewing anxiously Tabby called out: "I heard the sound of breaking crockery, Tommy!" And indeed, there were broken pieces all over the floor. This was bad luck! They had not noticed that a cup and saucer had been standing on the table. Tabby looked at Tommy with sad eyes and said in a sorrowful tone: "Do you think that our master will be very angry with us, Tommy?" Tommy shook his head and replied: "I'm not quite sure, but it is very well possible, for I believe that he was very fond of this cup and saucer, Tabby!" Tabby scratched behind her ear and then said: "We'll have to hope for the best."

It was lovely weather the next day and Tabby said

to Tommy: "Shall we go for a walk in the garden? I believe that Mrs. Duck and her little ducklings are out there as well." Tommy, who was always very ready for some fun, thought this was an excellent idea. When they got outside in the garden, the ducklings greeted them with a loud and cheerful quacking: "Hello, Tabby! Hello, Tommy! How nice of you to come and join us!"

But what was this they saw on the ground? It was their master's hat. Tommy picked the hat up with his mouth and said to Tabby: "Now you go and find what you can and put it in the hat. That will be fun!" Tabby and the little ducklings thought this was a grand game and they came running along with all sorts of things: sticks, old bones and stones. Of course this was not a very clean sort of game to play and the master's hat was beginning to look very dirty. How angry he was when he found out! Several days later Tabby and

Tommy were having another walk in the garden and they hoped that they would have some exciting adventures as life at home had been very dull of late. Tommy suddenly nudged Tabby and said to her: "Just look over there in the distance! What kind of funny fat animals are they?" Tabby laughed and called out: "Don't you know, Tommy? They are piglets!" Tommy nodded and said: "They are having a good meal from their trough. I feel hungry and would not mind joining them in their meal." He stood still for a moment and rubbed his paw over his tummy. "Yes", Tabby said, "now that you mention it, I feel that my tummy is empty too. It is such a long time ago that we had something to eat." Carefully Tabby and Tommy came nearer. Unfortunately they had to stop at a gate and the piglets were on the other side. "It seems we cannot get any closer", Tommy said and it was easy to see that he was very disappointed. "Never mind",

Tabby said. A week later Tabby and Tommy were walking in the garden when they suddenly made a great discovery. What was their great discovery? Well, they found a beautiful ball. They did not know whose ball it was, or how it had got there, but that did not really matter. The main thing was that the ball was there. Tommy at once jumped right on top of it, barking loudly. Tabby warn-

ed him and said: "If you make so much noise, then a lot of others will come along and they will surely want to play with the beautiful ball as well." Tommy replied: "You are quite right, I must keep quiet." But is was too late as Mrs. Duck was walking along already and she was not very pleased that Tabby and Tommy had such a beautiful ball. She was very jealous and what do you think she did? She tried to peck a hole in the ball with her beak, but that wasn't very easy. Tabby said; "If you do not get in our way too much, you may join in our

game." That afternoon Tommy went to visit his uncle, so Tabby went for a walk in the garden all by herself. But she hadn't been in the garden very long, when she heard: "Woof! Woof!" It was Tommy. His uncle Mr. Poodle hadn't been at home and therefore he quickly went to look for his friend Tabby. Tabby thought this was so nice of him, that she took a big jump and landed right on Tommy's back. They walked along like this for a short while, when Tommy stopped all of a sudden. And there in front of them stood. . . four sweet baby-chicks, who looked at him and Tabby in great surprise. "Hello, Mr. Dog", one of the chicks said and another one called out: "Hello Miss Pussy-cat". Tabby and Tommy spoke very kindly to the little chicks, but suddenly Mr. Cock came running along. He was very angry and he crowed out loudly that Tabby and Tommy wanted to harm his little chicks. Mrs. Hen, who was standing beside him said: "Yes, I think so

too!" They were both wrong however, as Tommy was a good little dog and Tabby really was a very kind pussy-cat, who never did anyone any harm. She even got along quite well with all the birds and the mice, but one day the brothers Mouse began to tease Tabby. This was very naughty of the brothers Mouse as one should never tease anybody. Nibble, who was the naughtiest of the Mouse family, was also the leader of his brothers. They kept throwing small bits of cheese and tiny stones at Tabby's nose. Oh dear, this made Tabby very angry. She said that she would give Nibble a good hiding if she caught him. Tommy, who had just finished telling a story to the baby-chicks, warned the little mice and said: "Little mice, stop this teasing right away as you will be

 sorry about it later on!" Tommy's words seemed to mean something to the litt-le mice and Nibble called to Tabby: "We will never do

it again, Tabby!" Tabby and Tommy were not always so very good themselves. Oh dear, no. If ever they were alone in the house, they made a great commotion. Tabby was very fond of milk and Tommy's eyes began to sparkle as soon as he saw or even smelt meat, especially sausage. One day when they were alone in the house, they discovered a bottle of milk and a delicious sausage on the table. Tabby looked at Tommy and Tommy looked at Tabby and they both had the same thought: "I wouldn't mind having something to eat!" Tabby jumped on top of the table and picked up the sausage. The sausage was for Tommy, but Tabby just had to have a little sniff at it herself. My, my, what a delicious smell it had! Tommy was getting a little impatient and barked: "Throw me the sausage, please, Tabby!" But what happened all of a sudden? Purely by accident Tabby had knocked the

bottle of milk over. All the lovely milk ran out of the bottle and on the floor. The brothers Mouse called out: "Now we can have a drink too!"

That afternoon Tabby and Tommy were playing round the dustbin. People had often told them that on no account were they ever to touch the dustbins. But... whenever they had a chance they seemed to forget all about this warning. They thought that a dustbin contained all sorts of things of great interest to a dog or a pussy-cat. Tommy soon found a lovely bone. There would no doubt be a nice fish-head in the dustbin for Tabby, but... she could not get in the dustbin very well. She wanted to push the lid right off, but Tabby was unfortunately not strong enough to do it by herself. Therefore she called to Tommy: "Tommy, please come and help me!" But Tommy was so busy with his bone that he didn't hear her. Mrs. Duck, who had also come along with her children to see if there were any titbits for her, said to Tommy: "Tabby

has just asked you something, Tommy. Will you go and help her, please. She cannot get the lid off the dustbin." Tommy grumbled: "I'll come and help her in a minute." A few days later Tabby and Tommy had a very exciting adventure. They had gone for a walk and suddenly found themselves in a garden, where they had never been before. They saw all sorts of things there without knowing what exactly they were. For instance there was a large wooden box. It was a queer box, as Tommy discovered that the lid of this box was on the side and it could be moved upwards. Tabby and Tommy just had to find out a little more about this box. May-be it was full of nice things to eat. Tommy jumped on top of the box, got hold of the lid with his teeth and pulled it upwards. What happened? Tabby and Tommy got frightened. Two animals with long ears jumped out of the box and ran away at great speed. In

great surprise Tabby and Tommy watched them disappear. They did run very fast! Mrs. Duck, who had seen all that had happened, said to Tabby and Tommy: "You have let the rabbits run away." The next day Tabby had a great surprise. She was enjoying a game with Tommy, the mice and the baby-chicks, when all of a sudden. . another pussy-cat appeared. Where had she come from? Tabby and Tommy really had no idea, but they did get very angry at the sight of another cat and they certainly were not going to allow her to stay in their garden. Tommy started to bark very loudly and Tabby began to spit and they made so much noise together, that it was most frightening. Therefore it is easy to understand that the strange pussy-cat felt anything but at ease and thought: "How can I possibly get away from here in safety?" In a timid voice she said: "I shall not do you any harm."

But nobody heard what she said and therefore she ran away as fast as she could. That evening Tabby and Tommy were out late in the garden. The moon was shining brightly and this was perhaps the reason why the baby-chicks could not fall asleep. Therefore they asked Tommy if he would tell them a nice and exciting story. Tommy thought for a moment and then he said: "Alright then, but you must promise me to go to sleep when the story is over." The little chicks nodded and together they said: "We promise you that we will do that, dear Tommy." Then Tommy told them a wonderful story about a very brave dog and a dear little pussy-cat. The baby-chicks listened without making a sound. What a good storyteller Tommy was! They would like to hear a story like this every night. And then they fell asleep.